IMAGINE THAT

Licensed exclusively to Imagine That Publishing Ltd
Tide Mill Way, Woodbridge, Suffolk, IP12 1AP, UK
www.imaginethat.com
Copyright © 2020 Imagine That Group Ltd
All rights reserved
0 2 4 6 8 9 7 5 3 1
Manufactured in China

Written by Joshua George
Illustrated by Dean Gray

ISBN 978-1-78958-484-4

A catalogue record for this book is available from the British Library

Not Another Squeak!

Written by Joshua George
Illustrated by Dean Gray

In the Faraway Wood,
under the tallest of trees,
Was the little mouse house
of a mouse family.

And in that small house,
where the big river bends,
Lived a mouse who loved talking
and making new friends ...

On the path by the river,
where bees buzzed around,
The mouse saw a bottom
that was big, fat and round.

'Well who have we here?'
said the curious mouse.
'I've never seen anyone
like you near my house!'

'Now just let me think ...
I suppose you're a bear?'

'Yes of course I'm a bear.
And I paw, and I snore and I ROAR like a bear!'

'Well how lovely to meet you,'
said the friendly grey mouse.
'I can't wait to tell everyone
back at my house!'

By a bush where the berries
grew as big as his head,
The mouse saw something move,
that was fluffy and red.

'What a marvellous tail!'
said the curious mouse.
'I've never seen anyone
like you near my house!'

'Now just let me think ...
I suppose you're a fox?'

'Yes of course I'm a fox,
I've got a big bushy tail
and little white socks.'

'Well how perfectly charming,'
said the friendly grey mouse.
'I can't wait to tell everyone
back at my house!'

By a clear and cool pool,
that was brimming with fish,
The mouse saw two eyes
watch each splash and each splish.

'Good gracious, who's this?'
said the curious mouse.
'I've never seen anyone
like you near my house!'

'Now just let me think ...
I suppose you're a cat?'

'Yes of course I'm a cat,
A cat does what he wants, and that is that!'

'Well a cat, fancy that,'
said the friendly grey mouse.
'I can't wait to tell everyone
back at my house!'

High up in a tree,
where the branches go creak,
The mouse saw some feathers,
and a sharp yellow beak.

'Well, hello up there!'
called the curious mouse.
'I've never seen anyone
like you near my house!'

'Now just let me think ...
I suppose you're an eagle?'
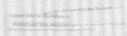

'Yes of course I'm an eagle,
I'm the king of all birds and I'm terribly regal.'

'What luck, a real eagle,'
said the friendly grey mouse.
'I can't wait to tell everyone
back at my house!'

In a bright sunny clearing
by a small grassy mound,
The mouse saw a body
that went around and around ...

'You're ever so long!'
said the curious mouse.
'I've never seen anyone
like you near my house!'

'Now just let me think ...
I suppose you're a snake?'

'Yes of course I'm a snake,
I hide, and I slide, and I glide like a snake ...

... and I'd rather eat a mouse than a nice piece of cake!'

But the little grey mouse
did not stop to chat ...

... with the bear, fox, or eagle,
the snake or the cat!